Forever Winter

Amber Daulton

Excerpt from Forever Winter

"I love you, Susanna Lorican. Nothing will change that." He clasped her tear-stained cheek in his palm. "Stay strong for me. We will get through this."

Guilt overwhelmed her. Susanna squeezed her eyes shut and pried herself from his arms. She needed space and time to think. As he tried to hold her hand, she shifted from his grasp and scooted as far back on the sofa as possible. Tears leaked from her eyelids. "It's all my fault." She stared up at Camden as another sob clogged her throat. She felt so unworthy. Foolish. She clutched her hands in her skirts and forced down the sob. "I'm sorry. What was I thinking? A winter wedding? I must be insane."

Dedication

To my husband: Thank you for your love and support, especially for dinner during the long nights when I disappear into another world.

Look for Amber Daulton's Other titles with Books to Go Now

A Hero's Heart

Lightening Over Bennett Ranch

Montana Ranch Collection

Mistletoe in the City

Handmade for Christmas

ISBN-13:978-1508723110

ISBN-10:1508723117

CHAPTER ONE

Southern Derbyshire, England

Christmas Eve, 1834

"Of all things, on all days." Susanna Lorican rubbed her throbbing temples. "Why now? What did I possibly do to deserve this?" Tears welled in her eyes. She hated the injustice. Months of preparation ruined! Stomping to the largest window in her bedchamber, she pushed open the protective glass panels and stumbled back. An icy gust rushed into the room. Embers crackled in the hearth. A chill spiraled down her spine and goosebumps marred her skin. She grabbed hold of the windowsill and stared outside, eyes burning until the gust changed course.

Her heart clenched as her fists tightened.

Sheets of downy white fell from darkened clouds and blanketed the rich, fertile countryside, sheathing acre upon acre of prosperous farmland. Billowing gray clouds concealed the early morning sun as the wind howled and blew snow in all directions.

She wouldn't mind a snowstorm on any other day—*or week.*

Activity below her second-story window caught her attention. A gasp lodged in her throat. Dreaded white covered the barns, stables and gardens. Several stable hands toiled in the cold to keep pathways clear around her father's stately manor. Luckily, the dirt road that led from town to Lorican Manor was still visible. If the snow continued, however, it wouldn't be visible for long.

Susanna stepped back from the window and

slammed the panels shut. Despising the floral wallpaper and ivory furnishings decorating her chamber, she imagined the rich colors and dark wood that decorated her future husband's bedchamber—*their* bedchamber. She had dreamt of that particular room far too often. Even though she toured his estate twice throughout their engagement, *his* bedchamber was strictly off-limits, thanks to the efforts of her parental chaperons.

She growled beneath her breath—an unladylike habit—but she felt too stressed to care. She flung her head back in frustration. "One day. All I needed was *one* day."

"Now, Susanna," a gentle, chastising voice soothed from across the large chamber. "The tiniest thing could have plagued us today and your temper would flare like hot coals. Fretting over the weather is useless. As long as the road remains travelable, all is not lost."

True, Susanna silently consented. She crossed her arms and stared irritably at her demurely dressed mother who sat on the edge of her rumpled bed.

Always soft-spoken and proper, Lady Marie Lorican was the epitome of class and beauty.

Susanna, on the other hand, her mother's youngest daughter, felt destined to always disappoint. No matter how hard she tried, she would never be as proper or as beautiful as her mother—especially since she couldn't seem to rein in her curses and reckless temper.

"I've waited so long, Mama. I want to marry the man I love." She sighed heavily and stared down at her cotton bedclothes. A faint blush stole into her cheeks. Tonight, if everything didn't fall apart before her very eyes, she would share a bridal chamber with her new husband and finally wear the lacy silk gown she'd secretly purchased in London a few months earlier.

Still, no matter what she wore, the eyes of her betrothed always gleamed in appreciation.

Lady Lorican clasped her hands together. Her thoughts followed Susanna's. "I will not waste my breath on preparing you for *wifely* duties that you understand too well already." Her pointed stare met her daughter's.

Susanna blushed scarlet and diverted her sky blue eyes to the floor.

Lady Lorican smoothed out a nonexistent wrinkle in her beige skirt. "Things happen. You and Lord Beckinworth will marry. Preparations have already begun to ready the main hall for the ceremony." As her daughter frowned, Marie huffed slightly in triumph. "I know you wanted to marry in the courtyard, but, as I have said, it is highly untraditional. A church is more favorable. You should postpone the wedding."

Susanna shook her head. Dark, unkempt tresses swirled around her face. "Today! We will marry today if it's the last blasted thing I do." She clenched her fists until the knuckles whitened. She struggled to stay in control of her emotions. "No amount of snow, ice or even hail will ruin this day." Stomping to her vanity and grabbing a brush, she forced the coarse quills through her thick mane and grunted as tangles snagged in the bristles. Her mother hurried to stand behind her and took the brush. She gently freed the tangles until locks of brown silk waved across her daughter's strong shoulders.

Susanna breathed deep and smiled into the vanity mirror at her mother Lady Lorican smiled in return. Her mother was right. Snow was nothing to worry about. As long as the reverend arrived safely to perform the ceremony, nothing could truly ruin her long-awaited day.

Susanna glanced at the diamond ring on her finger. As long as she had Camden Beckinworth, she needed nothing more.

****

"You are to be her husband. You tell her." Baron Alban Lorican poured himself a glass of brandy, drained it, and refilled the glass. He filled another and cast his gaze over his shoulder. A cursing young man sat hunched over in a comfortable leather chair with his head between his legs. He rocked back and forth. Lord Lorican stalked toward him, kneed his shoulder for attention and waited until their eyes met. Resignation darkened the younger man's brown gaze. Lorican handed him the second glass full of crisp, burgundy liquid and set the crystal bottle in front of him on the coffee table. "Drink up, my boy. You'll need it. In case you haven't noticed, that little lady has a temper like an ox."

Viscount Beckinworth's brow rose. He drained the glass, visibly shivered and closed his eyes. Seconds passed before he grabbed the bottle for a refill. "Believe me, I have firsthand knowledge of that temper. I even bear a scar to prove it." He rubbed at a small mark on his cheek and smiled. The woman amazed him in so many ways. "Besides, you are to blame for that, my lord. Lady Lorican is far too kind."

Lord Lorican huffed in a mixture of agreement and annoyance. He reclined in his favorite winged-back chair, lit a cigar and shook his head. "As I said, you tell the filly."

Camden nodded. The newest problem wasn't

major in the slightest, for the men at least. The women, however, would undoubtedly make mountains out of molehills. Tunneling both hands through his hair, he ripped out the ribbon pinning his long hair respectably to his nape and considered strangling himself with it. Refastening it, instead, he refused to take the coward's way out.

It was their wedding day. He shouldn't even see the bride beforehand. But, alas, what choice did he have? Send a servant in his stead? No. That poor soul didn't deserve his woman's temper for simply relaying a message. Besides, the manor was in turmoil. Every servant was hard at work preparing for the morning nuptials, not to mention the normal household duties. The storm couldn't have come at a worse time.

Spending several minutes with the baron in his immaculate study, Camden savored his second glass of brandy and a cigar before summoning the courage to speak to his betrothed. After appreciated but useless advice from the stressed baron, he headed toward the ladies' parlor where he expected his future wife to be relaxing. Instead, he found the cozy little room empty. *She must still be in her bedchamber.* Biting his lip, he contemplated visiting her there. While engaged, they were not yet married. It was completely unacceptable.

But rakes were expected to ignore propriety— even reformed ones, from time to time.

Bypassing several rushing servants chatting about the cold and winter plants, he headed upstairs as if he belonged. And he did, somewhat. The Loricans treated him like family even without marriage vows. He was forever grateful. His parents died five years earlier while he was away on the Continent. An only child without aunts or uncles to call on, he had spent the past four years as a recluse. He didn't know his parents had driven the Beckinworth name into the ground until he began sorting through his parents' debts, liens on the family estate and failing business. Thankfully, their bad business decisions did not affect his inheritance. Once everything was in order, debts and liens paid off, the business thriving, and his money properly managed, he decided to re-enter society and find a wife.

Luckily, he wasn't the same carefree man he used to be. He wasn't a fool to throw away the name, land and fortune he had built from ruin on a conniving or doltish woman. There were many stipulations that a woman had to meet to become the next Viscountess Beckinworth.

Attending a Christmas party last year at the estate of his parents' last true friends—the Loricans—he stumbled upon Susanna in the courtyard. She rested on a cobbled stair and held her foot, cursing under her breath. Once she noticed him, a blush stole into her cheeks and she instantly apologized for her foul language. Embarrassed, she explained that she played a game with the children and fell down a short flight of steps. The children left to find help. As he tried to help her to feet, she grimaced in pain and fell back on her bottom. Camden knelt beside her and grasped her ankle, covered by wool stockings. She gasped in pain but allowed the inspection. Without pulling down the stocking, he determined that her joint was slightly swollen and muscles tender. She had twisted her ankle.

Despite her protests, Camden picked her up and carried her close to his chest. The feel and weight of the supple woman stirred something primal in his blood. They had known each other for years but he never viewed her as anything other than the sister of his old playmates. But as she irritably folded her arms, humiliation flushing her face, he found himself wanting to kiss away her adorable frown. As a gentleman, though, he refrained. Winding through the courtyard, they reached the manor just as Lord Lorican, two servants and the nervous children hurried toward them.

Fortunately, after her ankle was wrapped in linen and she'd downed a glass of steaming tea, she rejoined the party, determined to have a good time. He spent more time with her than appropriate, but since she was unable to dance, his presence passed as nothing more than a family friend keeping her company in the midst of several peers and chaperones. He told her stories of the places he'd been, the people he'd met and made her laugh, distracting her from her sore ankle. That night, after her father's yearly Christmas Eve party dwindled into the wee hours of the morning, he surrendered to temptation and stole a kiss under the mistletoe that hung from the library light fixture.

Susanna was perfect in every way: honest, sweet and adoring, passionate, intellectual and stubborn. He had never known a woman like her. She exceeded every stipulation.

Camden paused at the top of the stairs and gripped the elegantly carved banister. His eyelids fluttered closed. He still remembered that moment in the library. Her lips parted into an innocent pout and blue eyes widened as he kissed her. Her breath caught in her throat and the hitching sound crawled through his stomach and twisted around his groin. But then sparks ignited in those docile blues and she pushed him back. Her hand slapped the entire length of his cheek. He didn't realize her nail cut him until later. He then nodded to the discreet mistletoe hanging over their heads. Her bashful grin silenced every roguish line he had ever used on a woman. And the blush stealing into her cheeks made him want to possess her, care for her and love her until the day he died.

Never in his life had he felt anything so profound or powerful. He knew, right then and there, he could spend the rest of his life with her.

As a few maids scurried by, jostling him out of fond memories, Camden focused on the task at hand. Stalking down the hallway richly garbed in winter greenery, berries, red and white ribbons and candles of all shapes and sizes, a mischievous smile softened the firm line of his mouth.

For several months, he had been a perfectly respectable suitor until one night changed everything. Visiting the Loricans for dinner, a thunder storm kept him from returning home. After spending an hour with the baron in his study, he retired for the night, but instead of seeking the guestroom, he found himself outside Susanna's bedchamber. Perhaps he had a little too much to drink, or was just desperate to see her, and he knocked on the door. When she answered, dressed in a modest robe that concealed every curve he wanted to sample, he couldn't deny the hunger burning in his blood any longer. He entered, shut the door behind him and kissed her. She didn't protest.

But when Lady Lorican accidentally walked in on them that morning, he thought everything was over. Or, at least, the wedding date would drastically be moved up. But the baroness simply diverted her gaze and walked out. She never mentioned a word of it—to him, at least. Susanna was another story.

It was a wonder her mother still treated him with any kindness or respect. Even more so that she didn't tell her husband about the compromising position she'd caught them in.

He shook the thoughts from his mind and headed for her bedchamber. Just as he was about to knock on the sturdy door, it swung open and the loveliest face he had ever seen scowled at him in shock. Then a loud shriek echoed past her lips and she ducked behind the door.

"Camden, why are you here? Do you wish for bad luck? The blasted snow is already an omen!"

Camden simply stood in the hall with his fist still raised to knock. Lady Lorican softly hissed at her daughter's language from somewhere within the room before she approached the doorway and invited Camden inside. He breathed a sigh of relief. Marie Lorican's presence established proper decorum even though just *seeing* the room where his betrothed slept and dressed was highly inappropriate. Politely nodding to his unexpected hostess, he noticed that panic devoured his bride's gaze.

"Now, Susanna." He held up his arms as Lady Lorican closed the door. "Before a string of unladylike curses flies from your lips, I'll explain. The—"

Susanna huffed and stomped toward him. She poked him in the chest and sniffed his breath. "You've been drinking and smoking this early? I bet my father is to blame. Even so, I thought you could abstain for one morning, you selfish, rude, irresponsible cad! You shouldn't be here!"

A deep breath expelled from Camden's lungs. She was right, of course. The blasted chit was always right. "I know, love. I apologize. But I am relaying a message from your father. You need to know there's been a slight change of plans."

She sighed as if his message was unimportant. "I already know about the snow. I know the ceremony must be inside. It doesn't matter to me." She shrugged her shoulders as if the situation was just an annoyance.

Camden's brow arched. Even though the snow started to fall at daybreak, it wasn't a blizzard. Thankfully, the clouds weren't dark enough for one. Still, he expected her to be more upset than just annoyed.

"There's something else." He glanced at Lady Lorican as sudden dread filled her gaze. Susanna's eyes widened with worry and she clutched her hands behind her back. He licked his dry lips and focused on Susanna. "Besides the storm." He coughed to find his voice. "We just received word that the dressmaker in London cannot deliver the dress or accessories. The bridges leading outside the city are iced over. It's too dangerous for the seamstress and her employees to travel here."

He caught Susanna as she stumbled backward. He helped her to the nearest chair and gently kissed her forehead.

She clasped her pounding chest in shock. "My—my dress... Not here? It should have arrived hours ago, late last night as scheduled." Her eyelids fluttered closed, and then snapped back open. Blue fire sparked like fireworks from them. "It should have arrived two weeks ago but the ignorant seamstress scheduled the wrong date. Last night was the earliest she could have it delivered." Susanna breathed deep and gagged softly on faint candle smoke that filled the room. "We must fetch my dress. Are the bridges really so dangerous?"

Camden knelt beside her and grasped her hand. "If conditions were good, it would take several hours by horse and carriage to reach London, load the chests and return; you know that. In this weather, it is impossible."

Susanna nodded even as tears beaded under her lashes. She abruptly swished her hand in the air to dismiss her own foolish question.

Camden wrapped his arms around her as her mother waited across the room by the hearth to allow them privacy. He tugged softly on Susanna's silky braid and kissed her forehead. "Calm down, love. You have several beautiful dresses. Choose one. You will look radiant, I promise."

"*Choose one?*" She pulled back, flabbergasted. Her eyes narrowed to thin slits. "This is my wedding dress we are discussing! Not apples. Not books. *My dress!* I cannot just choose another." She shoved out of his arms and stormed across the room. "How can I wear a dress if you've already seen me in it? It should be a surprise!"

"And it will." Camden stood and slowly approached her as she paced like a frantic tiger. "Only a few sets of clothes are packed for the honeymoon. Most of them are still in your armoire." Which were to be later delivered to Beckinworth Manor as they honeymooned in Paris. "Choose a dress you haven't worn in a while and do not tell me which. When you walk down the aisle, I will be surprised. I swear it."

Camden thumbed away her tears as she nodded. He knew Susanna had designed that damned wedding gown herself. Months of sketching and coloring, discussing details with a *supposedly* respected seamstress, were all wasted. She had been looking forward to this day for months. *Years.* He wanted nothing more than to strangle the seamstress for the mishap.

As Susanna forced her wayward emotions under control, determination blanketing the sadness in her eyes, Camden kissed her hand, nodded respectfully to her mother and left the women's company. Alone in the hall, a short, stressed laugh crawled up his throat and nearly strangled him. He swallowed hard. Even though the conversation went better than expected, his stomach still churned with anxiety. Something else was bound to go wrong.

He could almost feel it.

CHAPTER TWO

Camden assisted the baron with his daily business while Susanna and her mother spent the next few hours choosing a dress and matching accessories. He appreciated the time alone with the baron. He reminded him very much of his father.

"Have a seat, my lord." Lord Lorican offered Camden a chair as they returned to his study from the barn. The baron sat at his desk for several minutes and jotted down notes in various journals.

Camden jostled the dying embers in the hearth with a poker before relaxing in the same leather chair as earlier. He leaned his head back and closed his eyes, wondering which dress Susanna chose. As the smell of cigar smoke wafted through the air, Camden lifted his head and found Alban Lorican sitting across from him in his winged-back chair. When the baron offered a cigar, Camden shook his head. He only smoked when upset.

"Susanna is my youngest daughter. She is most dear to me." Lord Lorican glanced at a family portrait he had commissioned a few years ago that hung between two bookshelves. "She was never docile like her sisters. She acted just like her brothers. The boys, however, never threatened to give me a heart attack." He laughed and tunneled a hand through his dark hair. "I suppose I am to blame. When my last son left for Eton, I encouraged her hoyden ways by treating her as his replacement."

Camden smiled. "She always followed me around like a puppy when my parents and I visited Lorican Manor, or your family visited us. To tell you the truth, I thought of her as a pest. Back then, a difference of eight years in age felt like decades." He tapped his fingers on the armrest in thought. "I never expected us to marry. Foolishly, I expected her to remain a child, innocent and without need of a husband, even though Susanna was nearly grown by the time I returned after my parents' carriage accident." And it wasn't until last Christmas that he realized she was a woman, not a child, with a body that fulfilled his wildest dreams.

"Really?" The baron's eyes twinkled. "She was six when she first vowed to marry you. I believe her words were: *'Even if I have to hogtie him and drag him to Greta Green'.*" He laughed again as surprise flushed Camden's face red. "When you left for Eton—I think she was ten—she cursed you high and low for weeks. It was obvious to Marie and me—and your parents—that it was just a matter of time. And with her two disastrous

London seasons, money wasted and reputations embarrassed, we counted on a proposal from you."

"Glad to be of service." Camden grinned and stared at the portrait, completed when Susanna was about fifteen. Now twenty, the pesky little sister of his two best friends had grown into a lovely young woman. It warmed his heart to know his parents approved of his marriage.

"Now, with old memories aside, you deserve a fair warning, Camden." Lord Lorican sighed heavily and set his cigar aside in a bronze ashtray. "Obligation required me to warn my other future sons-in-law and now, even though my speech suited them far better than you, I still feel obligated." He crossed his arms over his stomach and glowered at Camden. "Men are known to stray in relationships. For some, the act is natural." The baron held up his hand as Camden started to protest.

"Your private life is not my business, but you will no longer be welcomed in my home if you physically harm Susanna. You will no longer be my son. If the abuse is so bad that she files for divorce and the courts grant it, I will stand by her decision no matter the scandal. Divorce is rare and expensive, but does happen. Never think that it is not an option." Air whizzed through his teeth in finality. "So treat her with care and respect."

The corners of Camden's mouth quirked up in a small smile. "You have my word no harm will come to her. She will never want for anything. I've known her for too long, I love her too much, to act a fool." He glanced down at his hands and stroked the finger that a gold wedding band would soon circle. "Susanna would be devastated if I took a mistress. She understands how society works—that it is acceptable—but she doesn't agree with infidelity, and neither do I."

Lord Lorican nodded in approval and relaxed. "Another warning…" The baron glanced at the journals on his desk. "I believe I mentioned this a few months ago but I am losing my best farm manager—my *only* manager—with this marriage. While the bride's price was quite satisfactory, it doesn't replace her skill."

Camden smirked while the baron's eyes twinkled in mischief. Susanna had obviously inherited her mischievous trait from him. "True, but you agreed to my terms. With her dowry and business skills, I have gained substantially from this union." Camden crossed his arms and flashed a smug smile, the legal business of the marriage contract finalized months before.

Lorican shook his head in laughter. "Anyway, my boy, Susanna will undoubtedly stick her nose in the journals and logs for your cotton mill."

He nodded. "I look forward to her opinion and

input." He had no wish to restrict her business pursuits and need for knowledge. "If she is as great a manager as you claim, I'd be a fool not to take advantage of her skills."

Once the serious conversation ended, they sat in peaceful silence for several minutes until Camden excused himself. Finding Susanna and her mother in the holiday-themed tea room—and since the custom of not seeing the bride before the wedding was already broken—Lady Lorican invited him inside to join them for a light snack. Refusing the small pieces of remaining bread, he sat beside Susanna and commenced with idle chitchat until a nervous servant appeared at the doorway.

The maid waited for the baroness to nod before she spoke. "Your presence is requested in the reception hall, milady."

"Very well." Lady Lorican sighed and rose from her comfortable chair. "Jane, dear, I need you to remain as chaperone."

"As you wish." Jane retreated to the farthest corner of the room once the baroness left to advise the other servants preparing the main reception hall—a large but stuffy hall with portraits of past relatives cluttering the walls.

Camden arched a brow. She had chosen a chair behind the sofa along the far wall, out of sight of their faces and body language. With this semblance of privacy, he grasped Susanna's hand as she idly toyed with the gloves she removed to enjoy the bread. Her gaze rose as she turned to face him. She batted her eyelashes.

In the presence of a chaperone, typically a married woman like Jane or one of Susanna's male family members, they acted coy and courteous. In the presence of her mother, however, the baroness allowed small liberties society typically scorned.

After several minutes of polite conversation, Susanna finally laughed about the day's mishaps. Reclining on a floral-print, cushioned sofa, she tilted her head and grinned at him. She squeezed his hand. "Nothing can truly ruin today."

His brow quirked. "What about an ill-timed snowstorm or a special dress?"

She blushed. "Not even that, now that I've calmed down and accepted it." Susanna sighed and maneuvered free of his grip. She quickly fitted her gloves back on her hands and glanced away. "I apologize for earlier. I acted so childish when you said the dress couldn't be delivered." She met his gaze as shame darkened her blue irises. "If you thought I blamed you, please understand I did not. You were simply the messenger and I took out my frustrations on you. I'm—"

He reclaimed her hand and she quieted. "No apologizes, Susanna." Now that her gloves prohibited skin-to-skin contact in the presence of the chaperone, Camden brought her hand to his mouth and kissed her knuckles.

He wanted to stroke her fine-boned jaw and trace her dark eyebrows with the pads of his fingers. He wanted to kiss her lips, neck and chest until she moaned in pleasure. They had slept together only once, just two months ago—a mistake neither regretted—but that one night barely sated him. In fact, he yearned for her more than before. Alas, that was his punishment for claiming her innocence before they were wed. His gaze burned with a fire that made her blush and her chest heave. He silently cursed and retracted his gaze. They were not alone. The chaperone might notice the sexual tension spiraling between them at any second and speak up. Even though she was a servant, Lady Lorican had given her the right and honor to protect Miss Susanna's reputation at all costs, even from her fiancé on her wedding day.

Camden considered Susanna to be a beautiful, charming and independent woman. Susanna, on the other hand, considered herself merely attractive and an unsuitable mate for most men. But he wasn't *most* men. He appreciated her bluestocking passion for literature, art and science. He encouraged and challenged her at every opportunity. She was his equal. He wanted nothing less.

Camden suddenly shot to his feet as gruff, boisterous shouting ricocheted throughout the manor. Susanna clutched her pounding chest. "Wait," Camden ordered as she tried to rise. "Stay here."

Camden and their chaperone hurried to the door. Three burly men caked in snow carried an unconscious man down the hall, while several servants gossiped from the doorway of a storage room. Jane barked commands to the women and they hurried to obey Lady Lorican's personal maid. She left the couple, albeit hesitantly, to find the baroness. Camden followed the snow-clad men, demanding answers, as Susanna rushed to his side and gasped.

"Reverend Chauncey, milord," one of the tired workers explained as he shifted his grasp on the reverend. "His horse lost its footing on a patch of ice. The reverend hit his head." They reached the baron's study just as Lord Lorican rushed toward them from another part of the manor. The baron quickly waved Susanna and Camden away as the men lay the injured man on a large, comfortable sofa.

Camden pulled Susanna back down the hall as tears filled her eyes. Escorting her back to the tea room, he left the door wide open since their chaperone had left. Lady Lorican would undoubtedly be furious with Jane.

He didn't know what to say. What the hell was going on? Today, of all days! It seemed as though the entire world turned against them: snow everywhere, no gown, an injured reverend—who he prayed would be fine. Nothing seemed to go right.

As Susanna retreated to the sofa and wrapped her arms around her stomach, he clenched his fists behind his back. This was their wedding day! She should be glowing and excited, not crying and stressed over a situation she had no control over.

But fate obviously had other plans, their

happiness be damned.

****

Susanna trembled as sobs clogged her throat. Camden rushed to her side and wrapped his arms around her. His lips brushed across her forehead. His touch was too intimate but she didn't have the strength or desire to pull away.

"Breathe," he instructed. "There's more than one man of the cloth in Derby, in your family's parish. Another will be fetched."

Susanna shook her head and then fisted her hands in his frilled shirt and striped waistcoat, crying as if the world had tumbled down on top of her. He held her close for several minutes, murmuring sweet words in her ear. She finally glanced up, her eyes red and puffy, and swallowed hard to find her voice. "Reverend Chauncey's horse slipped on ice, so I doubt the road is travelable. I don't want anyone else injured on our account."

He nodded. "I love you, Susanna Lorican. Nothing will change that." He clasped her tear-stained cheek in his palm. "Stay strong for me. We will get through this."

Guilt overwhelmed her. Susanna squeezed her eyes shut and pried herself from his arms. She needed space and time to think. As he tried to hold her hand, she shifted from his grasp and scooted as far back on the sofa as possible. Tears leaked from her eyelids. "It's all my fault." She stared up at Camden as another sob clogged her throat. She felt so unworthy. Foolish. She clutched her hands in her skirts and forced down the sob. "I'm sorry. What was I thinking? A winter wedding? I must be insane."

She stood in frustration and paced about the

spacious, richly decorated room. Evergreen garlands intertwined with rosemary, ivy and holly hung from every corner and looped across the walls. Red and white candles decorated with ivy and ribbons adorned the fireplace mantel. Small white votives and decorative wreaths adorned the windows for the Advent season.

The entire house was decorated for the holiday and Susanna realized she had been nothing but a fool. Her dear father had canceled his annual party. The servants were busy preparing for her wedding, surely stressed with all the changes, when they should be spending as much time as possible with their children. And the *children*! Oh Lord, why hadn't she thought of them? There were at least a dozen, all under ten, living in the household. Plum pudding, gifts and Father Christmas should be the only things on their minds. She had stolen Christmas from them with her blasted wedding! How could she do something so terrible?

And now the reverend was injured. Several wedding guests might be trapped in the storm or stranded in nearby towns, or injured and alone on the road. Only a small number of guests arrived yesterday evening, prior to clouds darkening the sky.

Tears cascaded down her face. She never thought of herself as a selfish person. She just didn't realize her wants overshadowed others.

She needed to find her parents, postpone the whole affair and focus on Christmas for the children. But with preparations already underway and guests due to arrive before noon—if they could—everything already accomplished today would be in vain.

Susanna hated acting like a helpless ninny. She was stronger than that. Wiping away her tears and breathing heavily to calm her nerves, she refused to let wayward emotions control her. Even though her special day burdened everyone, nothing could mend her terrible mistake. Everyone just needed to trudge on and get through the day.

She met Camden's concerned gaze. He tried for months to convince her to wait for spring, but she wouldn't listen. Last Christmas had been magical, life-altering. The anniversary of their first kiss. Even though she was so startled by it that she slapped him, that single kiss swirled emotions and needs inside her she didn't realize existed. She quickly fell head over heels for Lord Camden Beckinworth and wanted to commemorate that special moment by pledging their love on the anniversary.

Even though she was ashamed of her actions, she couldn't lie to him when he asked what was wrong. He knew her so well. He knew, somehow, that something more than just a chaotic wedding day caused the cascade of tears down her face. She explained everything—how she felt and what she'd done wrong.

When sweet Camden wrapped his arms around her, Susanna collapsed in a heap of tears. He cradled her close, protectively, but didn't deny the facts to appease her guilt. She was grateful. She needed to bear the shame and frustration. It was hers to hold and he respected her enough to let her work through it. But she wasn't alone. His embrace proved it.

Susanna sniffled against his shoulder and lifted her head to meet his gaze. "I—I planned the perfect wedding but never figured anything might go wrong. I never thought of anyone but myself." She lowered her gaze in shame. "I would change everything if I could, but now it's too late. Too much is already underway." She sighed and rested her forehead on his chest. "I didn't think of the little moppets, and it barely snowed last year. I just assumed this year would be the same." She gritted her teeth and pulled back from Camden's soothing embrace. She wrapped her arms around her churning stomach and paced again.

As Camden clenched his fists behind his back, Susanna berated herself for upsetting him. He tried so hard to be patient and she knew he needed to hold her. Every fiber in his body probably urged him to snatch her arm, pin her against his chest and kiss her until she melted in a puddle at his feet. If it weren't for the dreaded gossip if someone walked in on them, she wished he would.

"You were right." Susanna rubbed at her aching temples. "Mama was right. I'm such a fool. I never listen to reason. A spring wedding would have been wonderful." She easily imagined colorful wildflowers, green meadows and a cloudless blue sky. "Still, with my luck, these catastrophes would have happened regardless."

"No, love." Camden laughed softly. "Something bad can always happen. Rain, wind... anything. The dress still might have been late. It might even have been stolen by highwaymen on the way here from London. The reverend still could've fallen from his horse on a solid, dry road. Anything could happen."

Susanna nodded. She still wouldn't look at him.

Camden stomped toward her and grabbed both her arms, forcing the end of her frantic pace across the gleaming hardwood floor. "Susanna, listen to me." He squeezed her arms harder until her wet gaze met his. He relaxed his grip. "The children are having a wonderful time. I've seen many of them run through the manor, laughing with excitement. They're more than excited for tomorrow—Christmas comes once a year, but a wedding is even rarer. They love you. Don't you know that?" He sighed as she ducked her head into the crook of his shoulder and neck. Billowing chestnut hair tickled his nose and her sweet, feminine scent filled his nostrils. He glanced toward the open doorway, ever wary of unwanted visitors, but circled his arms around her anyway. If he was smart, he wouldn't touch her at all. Better still, he should leave the room so a chaperone wouldn't be needed. As it was, he couldn't leave her so depressed and guilt-ridden. "They've never been to a wedding before. The lads and lasses are sad you're leaving, but excited for our celebration."

Susanna nodded. Of her brothers and sisters who married at Lorican Manor, none of them allowed servants or children of any social standing to attend. Susanna wanted everyone there.

It broke her heart to leave the little moppets. She loved them, too, and would miss them terribly. She had been present for almost every birth—albeit she watched through a crack in the door while her mother, a midwife and a few others helped the expectant mothers deliver precious life. She had sung lullabies and played games with them for years while their parents were busy elsewhere.

She adored babies and couldn't wait to start her own family.

"I'm glad you chose winter—Christmas time." Camden gripped the loose braid of her chestnut hair. "Even though the timing isn't great, considering everything that has happened, it's perfect for us." He gently grasped her chin and forced her face up. He brushed his lips across her eyebrows. "I want to get married on the day that everything changed for me. On the day I finally found the one woman I could love and cherish all my life. No one is more important to me than you." He suckled her pink lower lip between his teeth. A soft moan escaped her throat. He pulled back and stared deep into her eyes. "You are so kind, love. I wish you realized that. Enjoy today, no matter what, but if something else horrible happens and prohibits our union, God forbid, we will marry as soon as possible." He clenched his jaw against the idea of waiting.

Susanna nodded. Emotional but intelligent, she understood logic and common sense when she heard it. Sometimes, it just had to be pounded into her.

Camden stroked a stray hair behind her ear and lowered his mouth to hers. Air filled her lungs seconds before his mouth clasped hers. His talented lips tasted and teased hers. A moan gurgled in the back of her throat.

"Camden," she gasped his name like a plea once he finally pulled back for air. "The door is wide open and we are without a chaperone." She blinked several times to clear her clouded vision. She licked her lips and nodded to the entryway. "Anyone could see."

He smirked roguishly. "Let them. We are betrothed. Two people in love, who are about to wed, are expected to kiss."

"Kiss, yes," she whispered. "You, my lord, make love with your lips." Susanna suddenly flamed scarlet. Her eyes widened like saucers and the temperature in the room skyrocketed.

Camden laughed as his embarrassed fiancée fumed. An arrogant grin spread across his face. "Do I? You have never admitted that before."

She scowled, her cheeks so hot she could barely stand it. "Well, there are some things you shouldn't be privy to."

His smirk lengthened. "Really? I am honored that my bride appreciates the way I kiss. If she didn't, what kind of man would that make me?"

She smacked his arm. "There are eyes and ears everywhere, Camden. Especially today. I'm sure the servants are already gossiping that we are spending time together on the one and only day we shouldn't. It's bad luck." To make matters worse, the few guests that arrived the evening before were bound to hear the gossip. And since their chaperone left without permission, leaving them unaccompanied, she expected another servant to arrive any minute, courtesy of her mother.

Camden drew her into his arms and brushed his lips across her hairline. "I make my own luck." He blew softly in her ear. She shivered in response. "We control our destiny, Susanna, no one else. Besides, you have nothing to worry about. The one activity we shared truly worth gossiping about will never reach the light of day."

Her face flamed even hotter. Air escaped her lungs in short, choppy gasps as she remembered the way he touched and fondled her for hours. That wonderful *activity* made her feel as if she was the most cherished woman in the entire world. She despised double standards, as did Camden, but because her good name and reputation needed to remain protected in all areas, especially in high society gossip circles, they refused to make love again until their wedding night.

But now, with her wedding possibly postponed, she glanced at the open doorway one last time and pushed it from her mind. She embraced Camden with all her strength. She was so tired of denying the wondrous craving that pooled in her stomach when he was near. Kissing him as if her life depended on it, she felt his breath entered her mouth and traveled deep into her lungs. She tasted his strong, rich essence and nearly melted. Trailing her hands up the back of his neck, she pulled free the ribbon pinning his long hair respectably to his nape and buried her hands in the dark silk. His embrace soothed the anger, worry and misery burning inside her.

Camden responded with equal fervor. He clasped the narrow dip of her waist and massaged firm flesh sheathed beneath layers of restricting peach-patterned fabric. He growled low in his throat and bent at the knees to reach the lacy hem of her day dress. Lifting several layers of skirt to grasp her thigh, he silenced her shocked moan by deepening the kiss. Her warm skin flared hot beneath his exploration. He trailed his hand higher until Susanna finally broke free from their intense kiss and twisted free of his smoldering embrace.

She stumbled back and braced herself against the sofa. She felt deliciously exposed and wanton beneath his yearning gaze. Breathing heavily, blushing scarlet, Susanna scowled at her fiancé but couldn't find the desire to reprimand him. He rarely touched her like that. She loved when he did. With any luck, after tonight, they wouldn't have to restrain themselves any more.

CHAPTER THREE

A knock vibrated on the tea room door. Susanna glanced up just as she finished nibbling on a bit of bread while resting on the sofa. Camden stood by a window across the room and watched the snow fall. Even with an appropriate distance apart, she blushed in the presence of the male servant. Her mother obviously did not send him.

"Yes?" Susanna called out with an air of forced nonchalance. She dusted her hands free of bread crumbs and stuck her hands back through her leather gloves. The servant entered and nodded respectfully. "Lord Lorican requests Lord Beckinworth's presence, milady." He then focused on the viscount as the man turned from the window. "His lordship is in his study, milord."

Camden nodded. "Very well. Tell him I will be with him shortly."

The servant nodded and withdrew.

As Camden headed toward the door, Susanna followed him. He stopped and frowned at her. "He requested me, love. Not you. Stay here. I will not be gone long."

Her brow rose. "I must check on the reverend. I have known him for years. Even if he is incapable of performing the ceremony, I need to be assured that he is fine and that there will be no lasting damage from his fall." She couldn't bear the guilt if he was seriously injured or died. She grasped her bicep and grimaced. She had broken her arm years ago after being thrown from a mad horse. She understood how dangerous such falls could be.

He glanced into the hallway just as two servants hurried around the corner with lace overflowing from their arms. Camden discreetly grasped Susanna's arm and pulled her away from the doorway. "I will inquire after the reverend. Your mother will return shortly or a chaperone will arrive in her stead. I would appreciate it very much if you waited here with the door locked. I do not want you wandering about unaccompanied."

Her brow rose. "Door locked? Unaccompanied? This is my father's home. I will go where I please."

The viscount gripped her arm slighter harder. "Not today, Susanna. Listen to me for once in your life. As your future husband, I am asking that you wait." He released her without further discussion and left the room.

Perplexed by his strange behavior, Susanna irritably crossed her arms but did as her betrothed requested. Several minutes passed until curiosity chipped away at her patience. Stalking to her father's study, she pressed her ear to the door. Camden's voice, as well as her father's and a few other mens' echoed from within but she couldn't decipher their clipped words through the thick barrier.

With a long sigh, she returned to the tea room for the empty breadbasket and dropped it off in the kitchen. She then decided to find either her mother or her visiting sisters. Even though she cared for her two older sisters, she found them conniving and self-centered. They married for class and security, choosing the wealthiest men who made offers for them. Her brothers likewise married titled women with sizeable inheritances. While they all made excellent matches, love simply wasn't important to them. Her brothers sought mistresses soon after their nuptials and she believed her brothers-in-law did, as well.

After a year of courtship, six months of which were part of their engagement, Susanna still felt amazed that she had made a love match—with a viscount, no less. After two embarrassing London seasons, she expected to marry a commoner with a good supply of land and wealth. Love had little to do with marriage. She needed a husband to provide shelter, clothing and food. Men needed wives to bear children—preferably males—to ensure the continuation of their family name. Despite this, many fortune-hunters found her unsuitable since she was the fifth child of a baron. Her inheritance was modest.

Camden Beckinworth, now the fifth viscount of the Beckinworth estate, didn't care. While the handsome rake wasn't the sort she sought for a husband—with a reputation for adventure while at Eton and during his year on the Continent—she found the man beneath the flawed exterior to be vulnerable and sincere with a sarcastic wit. His surprising kindness and respect ensnared her heart early on. And though he could be arrogant to a fault, she found him down-to-earth with simple wants. She trusted him, and valued that even higher than love. He would never dally with other women. He would always protect her. If they fell on hard times, as had his parents, she wouldn't mind getting her hands dirty—literally, since he owned and operated an extensive cotton mill in northern Derbyshire. Commitment and vows should never be broken; for richer or poorer.

Unfortunately, her siblings and their spouses did not regard vows so highly.

Susanna growled softly beneath her breath as she thought of her eldest sister's husband. She doubted the scoundrel kept his marriage vows for more than a week. He flirted with her on far too many occasions for her to think of him in brotherly terms. Her sister did not believe her—and even called Susanna a useless, jealous child making unfounded accusations—and a rift separated them ever since.

She headed toward the main reception hall, anxious to see how her mother and the servants could possibly transform the stuffy hall into something airy and magical. Paying little attention to her surroundings, she turned the corner far too fast and slammed hard into something large blocking her path. Stumbling back, two strong hands easily caught her before she landed on her bottom. Susanna quickly composed herself before darting her gaze to a face that churned her stomach.

"Now, Susanna, what if I had been a servant carrying dinner or laundry? As lady of your own household, you must be careful."

The airy, laughing comment would have sent blush steaming into her cheeks had it come from anyone other than her sister's husband—her *eldest* sister's husband.

She stepped back and maneuvered free of his smarmy grip. Surprisingly, the tall, broad man in his early thirties allowed the retreat with a jovial smile plastered on his weasel face.

"Lord Gaynor, how nice you could come." Susanna inwardly cringed as she offered her hand for him to kiss. Luckily, she wore gloves. "You arrived last night, correct? Unfortunately, I already retired for the night and could not greet you." While her sisters and brothers arrived several days earlier with their families in tow, Earl Gaynor had been preoccupied. She considered it just another stroke of bad luck that he managed to attend her wedding after all.

He grasped her hand and kissed just above the knuckles. His smile widened until pearly white teeth, menacing like a wolf's, peeked out from his lips. "Today is special. I understood completely." He offered his arm to escort her down the hall.

Susanna gritted her teeth. She couldn't refuse without offending. He had done or said nothing offensive—yet. Besides, he was a guest in her father's home; she was obligated to be polite. As he led the way to the main hall, a few servants passed by with Christmas greenery in their arms. She breathed deep of the fresh evergreen and allowed the strong scent to soothe her.

"Are you nervous?" Lord Gaynor bent his head closer to hers, his voice a mere whisper.

Susanna shivered as his cool breath skated across

her cheek. "Nervous? Of course not. I am pleased to marry Lord Beckinworth."

Gaynor grinned. "My sweet Deandra was just as naïve and happy as you are now. All she could think of was the wedding."

Susanna remembered. Deandra's demands on her wedding day had been outrageous. "I doubt my sister was naïve five years ago, but I do believe she was happy. Is she still?" Susanna already knew the answer but her curiosity burned for his opinion.

He shrugged his shoulders. "Obviously. I am in no short supply of money." He lightly chuckled. "And the twins keep her and the governess very busy."

Susanna feigned politeness even though his words wounded her. Deandra was terribly unhappy. She was the mother of two spoiled children with a husband that frequented taverns and gentlemen's clubs. Deandra pretended nothing was wrong, even the obvious fact that her live-in governess was her husband's mistress. Susanna and her parents, and Camden, when he dined with them over the summer, pitied their happy façade. Everyone was miserable—except Lord Gaynor.

"The wedding," Gaynor continued, "was not what I meant. Are you nervous of what is expected of you afterward? Tonight?"

She frowned in confusion. A few seconds passed before her gaze widened and she stopped dead in her tracks. She whipped her smoldering gaze to her brother-in-law's. "That, my lord, is none of your business." Her temples throbbed and her blood pounded in fury. "Thank you for the escort but I can easily find my own way through my father's manor." She tried to jerk her arm free but he tightened his grip.

"Why, Susanna, I only ask out of reasonable

concern." He scanned the hall in both directions. Servants chatted in the distance but no one was near. "And now you are upset. Obviously, you must be worried. We should discuss it." He pulled her into the nearest room, an expansive library with large, airy windows now cluttered by obstructing wreaths and candles.

Susanna growled deep in her throat and wrenched free. She hated being alone with him. He made her feel weak and worthless. As he quickly closed the double doors and faced her, she braced both hands on her waist, refusing to appear weak or scared. "This is highly inappropriate." Even though she had spent time alone with Camden, and that was just as inappropriate as this now, *that* door had been open and she trusted Camden. In her mind, though perhaps not in society's, there was a difference. "Have you been drinking? You know this is improper."

Lord Gaynor simply smiled and motioned her to the nearest couch. She refused to budge. He remained in front of the doors. "Improper? Not at all. We are family and I am married." He glanced down at the gold band circling his finger. His gaze then encompassed the large chamber filled with scores of heavy, leather-bound books. "You are a respectable young woman and we should discuss your fears. If I can offer advice or assistance in any way, I would be honored to do so."

Her brows rose. The blasted man was incorrigible! They had never been close. And even if they were, she would never discuss such private things with a man!

A man not her husband.

The first time he touched her—an accidental grazing of her breast when she was sixteen—had left her wary of him. She convinced herself she imagined it; that he truly had lost his footing and bumped into her. But when it happened again, and this time his gaze connected with hers, fiery intention blazing, she knew to avoid him, to never be alone with him again. She should have told her mother the first time it happened. Or the second. Or the third or fourth. But she was too embarrassed. Not only that, the scandal would have publically humiliated her sister. Every time she visited her eldest sister, or Deandra and her husband visited Lorican Manor, Lord Gaynor always found reason to be alone with her. She couldn't escape him when everyone considered them friends. Family.

Once she finally summoned the courage last year and confessed everything to her sister, she had lost Deandra as a friend. But she didn't regret telling the truth. Deandra, as foolish as she was, deserved nothing less.

She thought of Camden and her thumping heart calmed. He would search for her once he returned to the vacant tea room. Several servants saw Gaynor walking with her, but would think nothing of it. After all, strolling through the hall where anyone could see them left them little privacy compared to behind closed doors where anything inappropriate could happen.

Unlike her sister, Camden believed her and promised to keep the bastard away from her. An impossible promise, but she hoped for it nevertheless.

Now that she was alone with Lord Gaynor, an important earl who lived in an immaculate estate outside London, she truly felt alone. This was her father's home, a place she should feel safe, and the library was her favorite room in the manor, but now everything felt alien.

As Lord Gaynor stalked toward her, she backed up and hurried around a delicately-carved lounger, placing it between them. Her heart pounded in her throat. She swallowed hard and jerked her gaze to the solid, sturdy doors, wondering if she could dart by him and escape. She knew there wasn't enough time to race to a window, toss the greenery and candles aside, thrust open the panes and somehow gather her wide, billowing skirts in her hands to jump out into the deep snow.

"No, you aren't nervous about tonight." Gaynor easily maneuvered around the lounger. "You have experience. I'm sure the viscount is grateful, but I highly doubt he would like that information spread. I have many connections, you know. All I have to do is tell a few certain people and the ton would be aghast."

She bit her lip. "You have no proof. Would you

like to be sued for slander? Attacking a proper lady's reputation without fact or merit is risky."

He shrugged his shoulders. "I am willing to take that chance, unless you find a way to convince me otherwise."

Susanna barely breathed as dozens of thoughts rushed through her mind. She wasn't virtuous, but he had no way of knowing it. He was testing the water, trying to break her by blackmail. She refused to fall victim, refused to allow his cold words to taint that night of passion she held dear to her heart.

"Be my guest, but expect a barrister and a Bow Street Runner on your doorstep."

He folded his arms across his chest in challenge. "You act innocent, but I doubt you are. Men have needs and waiting for a proper woman is torturous. Not that I know anything about that. Deandra was quite willing before our nuptials." He smirked as she cringed. "I do not see a man of Beckinworth's reputation waiting long. Perhaps he sought solace elsewhere? Do you know of his travels in Europe?" Triumph sparked in his eyes as she clenched her fists. "He was living with two prostitutes in Amsterdam when his parents died. He visited brothels all the time while at Eton. We often shared ladies, but rarely spoke outside idle chitchat."

Tears beaded under her lashes but Susanna used anger to push them back. She heard similar rumors and even mentioned a few to Camden. He admitted to them but promised those bachelor days were over. "I am asking you politely to leave me alone. I'm not a frightened little girl you can bully. Not anymore. If you do not step aside, right now, I will tell my father and fiancé about this. I will not keep this harassment quiet any longer."

His grin widened clear across his face. "I swear Beatrix was not this difficult." He cocked his head. "She barely argued the first time I cornered her. And now, even though she is married, she hungers for our occasional rendezvous."

Susanna felt sick. *Beatrix* had slept with him? She never would have imagined that Bea, the obedient, proper child, indulged in affairs. "I'm leaving. You will not follow me." Stomping around a reading desk as tears burned and threatened to fall, she knocked over a chair as he hurried after her.

Gaynor tripped, just as she planned, but still managed to wrap his strong arms around her and haul her away from the doors. Refusing to scream, and not wanting the entire household to witness the attack, she fought her captor and clawed at him with her nails. Cursing her gloves, she stomped hard on his foot, but he merely grunted.

Pinned helplessly against him, her head spun in disbelief. He laughed at her useless efforts and tossed her on the nearest sofa. She landed with a hard thud and cried out as the sharp edge of a discarded book jabbed her spine. She barely had time to shove the book to the floor before he jumped on top of her. He straddled her waist and grabbed her flailing arms to pin them at her sides. She kicked and thrashed, screaming for him to get off, uncaring that anyone could burst through the door and find them. In fact, she wanted someone to find them—she didn't give a damn about her reputation. He would force her, *rape* her, and she wasn't strong enough to stop him.

Pinning her arms with his knees, he painfully squeezed her breasts and trailed his hands down her torso as she hissed and cried out. Ripping the lace from her bodice, he forced his fingers beneath layers of fabric to grasp warm flesh. He pinched her nipple and shifted his knees to rub his crotch against her.

She jerked her hands free as his shifting knees loosened around her arms. Instead of shoving and pushing him off, Susanna ripped off her gloves and slashed his face, aiming for his eyes. Blood beaded across his cheeks in deep lines as he hauled back in pain. She grabbed the book and rammed it into his gut. Shifting sideways to loosen her trapped legs, she kneed him in the crotch and he fell to the floor. She scrambled to her feet but he tackled her, pinning her with his body and slapping her hard across the face.

She cried out just as the doors to the library crashed opened. The sound of stomping echoed in the chamber as several people rushed in. Hands pulled Gaynor off her. She clamped her legs together and scurried back. Tears welled in her eyes as Camden punched the bastard several times in the face. Gaynor collapsed on the floor, blood spewing from his mouth.

Her betrothed rushed to her side and pulled her into his arms. Susanna grasped him hard and buried her face against his chest, crying in panic and relief. He buried his hand in her messy braid and murmured soothing words, coaxing her to explain. Once she finally pried herself from his chest and stared over at Gaynor, who had risen to wobbly knees, she noticed that her father and three servants bore witness. Anger and confusion strained the baron's eyes. She lowered her gaze and quickly explained.

Gaynor fervently shook his head and clasped his aching jaw. "She coerced me into the library. She is very beautiful, and very persuasive. Shamefully, I lost all inhibitions."

With that, Camden launched himself at the earl and tackled him to the hardwood floor.

The baron ordered the servants to drag Camden off Gaynor just as Lady Lorican and Deandra rushed into the room. The women gasped as the men rolled on the floor, fists flying. The servants grabbed Camden's arms and pulled him back. Gaynor kicked out but missed the viscount's leg. Camden shrugged off the servants and rubbed at his sore jaw. Lady Lorican rushed to her crying daughter and held Susanna close.

Deandra hurried to her bleeding husband but he shoved her away. She scowled at the seething viscount but focused on her youngest sister. "What did you do? Tempt him?" Deandra hissed at Susanna. "My husband is loyal. He would never touch you!"

Susanna gripped her mother harder as sobs overwhelmed her. Both Susanna and Deandra cried as

Camden bristled and clenched his fists.

"Leave," the baron ordered the servants. "If you speak of this situation to anyone, consider yourselves jobless and your families homeless." The servants quickly nodded and left. Only the Lorican family remained. "Deandra, Susanna quiet. I cannot handle two emotional women with a blasted headache." He rubbed his temples and then stared at Lord Gaynor.

The earl tried to speak but his words slurred together. He wiped blood from his lips with the sleeve of his dark shirt and swallowed the excess blood pooled in his mouth. Gaynor rose to his feet as Deandra clung to his arm to keep him steady.

Lord Lorican crossed his arms and scowled at his son-in-law. "I believe my daughter. You cornered and attacked my child on the day of her wedding. You struck her, groped her and now deny it like a rat." He held up his hand as both Gaynor and Deandra tried to speak. "You may be an earl, my lord, but are no longer welcomed in my home. I will see that a doctor tends to your injuries, but you will leave once the roads are passable." He focused on his eldest daughter. His eyes softened but his tone was firm. "You are always welcomed here, as are your children, but not your husband." He ignored Gaynor as the earl fumed. "You have shown little love or respect for your sister. I thought better of you, Deandra."

Deandra wrung her hands. "My husband would never touch Susanna. Or Beatrix. Dallying with my sisters is one boundary he would never cross." Gaynor squeezed her arm for silence as she swiped at falling tears. "I admit my husband and I have marital issues, but I am certain this whole thing is a huge misunderstanding, Papa."

Lord Lorican glanced at Camden. The younger man nodded. The baron then licked his lips and sighed. "Lord Beckinworth and I have had long talks about your husband's actions regarding Susanna. I hoped what he had told me was nothing but tall tales, but after this, I believe him entirely."

Susanna frowned and flushed red. She met Camden's gaze.

"I'm sorry, love." Camden approached her but paused as she turned away. He clutched his hands behind his back and then met Lady Lorican's questioning, teary gaze. "She wanted it kept secret. Lord Gaynor made several innuendoes over the years. Several 'accidental' grazes, but nothing like this. No direct attack, as far as I know." He arched an eyebrow at Susanna. As everyone in the room stared at her, she nodded quickly. "If everything would have gone according to plan today, I would not have seen you until the ceremony. I couldn't have guarded or protected you. I told your father because I needed someone to watch out for you in my absence."

Susanna finally looked up to see shame fill his gaze. He obviously blamed himself for this predicament, but he shouldn't.

"Lord and Lady Gaynor," the baron said, "you are dismissed. We will speak later, my lord, at great length."

The Gaynors left. While Susanna didn't really expect better, she still felt betrayed that her sister believed her snake of a husband. She unwrapped herself from her mother and stood on wobbly legs. Camden rushed to her side and pulled her safely into his arms. Without a word, she flung her arms around his neck and kissed him.

Once Susanna pulled back and stroked his sore jaw, he kissed the crown of her head. "This was why I wanted you to wait for me in the tea room with the door locked while I spoke with Lord Lorican. I feared Lord Gaynor's actions if he found you without an escort." He then cursed his words as she lowered her head in fault. He lifted her chin with his finger and forced her to meet his gaze. "I shouldn't have expected you to listen to me without an explanation. Susanna, I do not wish to control you, but everything I say, whether I ask or order it, is for your own protection."

The baron kissed his wife's hand before folding his arms across his chest. "Do not fret about any of this, Susanna. It will soon be nothing but a horrible memory. There is, however, more bad news." He sighed as Marie stared up at him in concern. "We have to postpone the wedding. The road is now impassible with icy slush.

Several guests are likely stranded in Derby and other nearby towns. Luckily, one of the guests already here is a doctor. He gave Reverend Chauncey a clean bill of health but ordered bed rest. Because of the road we cannot call for another reverend."

Lady Lorican sniffed and wiped away tears.

"We don't have much choice, love." Camden brushed stray hair from Susanna's bruised cheek. A purple blemish formed beneath her eye. He clenched his fists and held her tighter. "We shall marry in a few months. We'll obtain another special license to have the wedding outside your family's parish. By then, the snow should be gone. You'll wear the dress you designed, the courtyard will be overfilled with spring flowers and everything will be much calmer."

Susanna pinched her eyes shut but nodded. She clutched Camden closer.

Camden then addressed her parents. "My lord, my lady, I wish to take her to her chambers. She needs rest." His gaze narrowed. "I understand my request is highly inappropriate but, given the circumstances, I do not care. Her well-being is my only concern."

Lord Lorican's brow rose as he glanced at his wife. Lady Lorican nodded. "Of course," the baron replied. "We trust you with her. Make sure my daughter rests and all her needs are met. Come by my study within the hour."

Camden agreed.

Susanna bit her lip. Gaynor held more power, prestige and money than either her fiancé or father. They would undoubtedly speak with the bastard in private and hopefully come to some kind of resolution. If not, a lawsuit could be on their hands.

She silently cursed, wishing she could just snap

her fingers and wake from this horrible dream. "Camden…" She peered up at him as he silenced her apology by placing his finger on her lips. The love, concern and protection that boiled like embers in his dark eyes burned through her defenses. God, she loved this man more than life itself.

The library doors suddenly burst open and her brothers rushed in, flanked by Beatrix, now heavy with child, and her husband. Susanna's eldest brother explained that they found Deandra crying alone outside her old bedchamber. They hastily sought out the library after she explained what happened, though still in denial of any wrongdoing on her husband's part. Each brother hugged Susanna, as did Beatrix. Embarrassment and shame darkened Bea's eyes. Susanna now believed Lord Gaynor lied and took advantage of her sister. They would have a long talk about that later.

Once the three men shook Camden's hand and Beatrix hugged him in gratitude, the baron's eldest son, the heir to the Lorican Barony, focused on his father. "Reverend Chauncey is awake. He is tired but determined to see the wedding through." He directed his gaze toward those in question. "Are you still willing?"

Susanna eagerly nodded as Camden sighed in relief.

Lady Lorican clapped her hands together. "There is still much to do. Camden, my son, I will take Susanna upstairs to prepare. You will speak with my husband, do what you must and then dress. Once the two of you leave this room," she narrowed her gaze on both her youngest daughter and future son-in-law, "there will be no more contact until the music plays. Beatrix, you will accompany us."

Beatrix nodded happily.

Once Marie Lorican gave orders, no one defied her. As her mother and sister pulled her from the library, Susanna glanced over her shoulder and met her betrothed's gaze. She wanted to stay, needing to know what the men decided regarding Lord Gaynor even though she had no control over the earl's fate. The day had been a complete disaster. She still felt frazzled and unsure of herself but as Camden mouthed the words, *'I love you'*, she focused on the only thing she now had control over—*the wedding*. She would finally get married. And it was about damned time.

CHAPTER FOUR

"Beautiful." Lady Lorican dabbed at tears beading under her lashes.

Beatrix clutched two of her favorite magazines to her chest: the *Ladies' Cabinet of Fashion, Music and Romance* and *The Court Magazine and Belle Assemblée*. Styling her sister's accessories and hair according to detailed descriptions, Susanna appeared every bit a model for a wedding fashion plate. "I'm so happy for you." The petite brunette beamed at her taller sister.

Susanna swished her skirts and giggled as she admired herself in the full-length mirror. She dressed in a pale pink and ivory silk ensemble, with short, yet puffy, Beret sleeves. Elbow-length white gloves graced her arms. A low, square neckline trimmed with lace fell off her shoulders. A satin band fit snug around her waist. Heavy skirts reached her ankles and were embroidered with silk near the bottom. Twisting her feet to admire her ivory stockings and square-toed heels, she didn't expect to appreciate—*adore*—the gown as much as she did.

With her long tresses swept up and decorated with ivy and holly, they draped a lace veil over her curled hair. Diamond earrings dangled low from her ears and a matching necklace shimmered under the light of the glowing hearth. Powder hid the blemish under her eye and natural blush filled her cheeks. Clear pomade added sheen to her lips.

A knock resonated at the door. Lady Lorican answered and her husband entered. He beamed with pride and took Susanna in his arms. He kissed her cheek before pulling back to admire her. "You look radiant. I feel so old, sweetheart. All my children are now wed. Well, soon. I expect more grandchildren by next year." He kissed Susanna's cheek again before releasing her to hug Beatrix. He petted her growing stomach and cooed to the unborn child. "Well, it's time. Reverend Chauncey has prepared for noon by tradition. We shall dine with a customary wedding breakfast and dance soon afterward."

"It's so unbelievable." Susanna clutched her shaky hands together and smiled. "I never thought this moment would come, especially after all the mishaps today."

"But none of that is important right now." Lord Lorican patted her hand. "You are lucky. Even though I detest the idea of arranged marriages, I would've chosen a spouse for you had another season in London been disastrous. I can only afford so many parties, balls and gowns." He laughed softly as she blushed. "Your brothers have been with Lord Beckinworth for the past hour or so, railing the poor man with their big brother speeches."

Her brow rose at a mischievous angle. Camden typically regressed into a callow youth when around her brothers. "I assume he received *your* speech earlier, too."

"Of course. I am your father." He grinned as Marie rolled her eyes. "I've never seen a man more excited, anxious and relieved than your viscount. You've chosen well for yourself."

"I agree."

Taking Susanna's arm in his, Lord Lorican led the ladies from the bedchamber to the vestibule outside the main reception hall. With Deandra out of the wedding, Lady Lorican took her place as a bridesmaid. As a few smiling servants handed the women extravagant bouquets of winter flowers adorned with ribbons, Lord Lorican stuck his head through the open archway and signaled the quartet he hired from Derby. Once soft music began to resonate through the large chamber, Lady Lorican entered one step at a time. Beatrix soon followed.

"Are you ready?" Lord Lorican whispered to his youngest.

"More than you know."

He peered down at her and tears shone in his eyes. "I am so proud of you. My little girl is getting married. I can barely believe it."

Tears glistened in hers. "I'll always be your little girl, Papa. And Beckinworth Manor is close by. You'll see us often. Besides, since you want many grandchildren, I will call on you and Mama for help all the time."

He laughed and hugged her close. "I look forward to it."

Once the soft sounds of the violin, viola, clarinet and cello deepened, Lord Lorican draped the veil over Susanna's face and hugged her. Then he straightened, patted his daughter's arm and led the way.

Passing beneath a richly adorned archway, mistletoe and ivy impressively looped within thick garlands, Susanna nearly stumbled. Air stilled in her lungs. The once stuffy and oppressive hall was now airy and breathtaking. Ivy, holly and red huckleberry hung from every lofty corner, intertwined with bright, imported amaryllis blooms and white ribbons. Spruce, laurel and galax leaves lay scattered about the floor and on the burgundy carpet beneath her feet. Lace, tulle and ribbons decorated tables and chairs. Ribbons and ivy dangled from gold sconces. Hundreds of white candles, large and small, glowed brightly.

At least three dozen people stood as Susanna entered, far more than she expected. Several were important guests from neighboring areas while many were from London. A fair number of servants stood near the back with their grinning children.

And then her gaze met Camden's. He stood before the reverend and the elegantly adorned hearth, the mantel trimmed with ivy, berries and tulle. Love and devotion beamed from his eyes. Dressed in a fashionable silver cloak with padded shoulders, a gray, double-breasted waistcoat, frilled shirt and stiffened gray cravat, strength and pride emanated from his muscular frame. Dove-gray trousers and dark leather shoes lengthened his long legs. A silver ribbon held back his silky brown hair. She had never seen him look more handsome.

Susanna wanted to run down the aisle, grasp him close and kiss him before the reverend uttered a word. No other man had ever made her feel so passionate. She longed for his touch, his kiss. She belonged to him and he belonged to her. This chaotic day proved it. Here they were, after every mishap, about to marry. Nothing could stop them.

Her heart pounded a ferocious rhythm. She barely heard the beautiful music. Barely breathed. She knew Camden had always considered himself strong and proud, a man who needed nothing and no one, but the longing in his eyes defied that knowledge. He needed *her*. And before she realized it, Susanna and her father were just feet away from him.

The baron smiled and placed his daughter's

gloved hand in Camden's, then stepped back and stood beside his grinning sons in the audience.

Susanna wrapped her arm around Camden's and felt him shudder. Heat flared in his eyes and she assumed it took all of his willpower to behave. As they approached the reverend, she lifted on her tiptoes to whisper in his ear. "Are you surprised about the dress?"

An amused grin split his lips. "Very much." A strand of ivy brushed across his nose as he leaned down to whisper. "The pink is perfect. You couldn't have worn a better gown."

Relief filled her face. The whispering couple quieted once they reached Reverend Chauncey. The tired, middle-aged man leaned against an elegantly-carved wood lectern but straightened at their approach. They nodded respectfully, *thankfully*, and as the music faded, the guests resumed their seats .

The reverend repressed a yawn and opened the large, heavy book sitting on the lectern to a particular passage. "I must say I am blessed to be here. After the snow and ice, this morning is truly special for all of us." Reverend Chauncey rolled his eyes toward heaven in gratitude. "I have known the bride and groom since they were wee ones. They deserve happiness— especially after today. Viscount Camden Beckinworth, the Honorable Miss Susanna Lorican, let us begin."

The next half hour passed in a span of minutes. Susanna listened attentively as the reverend spoke lovely words of hope and praise from his heart and recited from the antique Bible. The entire morning felt surreal. She half-expected another mishap. The rest of the ceremony or the upcoming breakfast could be potential disasters.

As Camden repeated the vows the reverend

spoke, he removed her glove and slipped a gold wedding band onto her finger. Their initials and wedding date had been inscribed on the inside of the band. He gently folded her glove and slipped it into his pocket while reciting his vows.

Susanna swallowed a sob of happiness. His heartfelt words meant the world to her. As the reverend focused on her, she managed to repeat his words through falling tears and slipped a similar band on Camden's finger. Words of love flowed from her mouth and heart, churning Camden's gaze with emotion.

Once the reverend pronounced them man and wife, every thought left her mind except one. She married him. *Finally!* A man eight years her senior, a young boy she once admired from afar, Camden Beckinworth was now hers! As Camden lifted her veil, she wrapped her arms around his neck and kissed him.

She couldn't help herself. She needed to feel him all around her and breathe the air he released from his lungs.

She heard the reverend laugh at her enthusiasm as Camden's arms circled protectively around her waist. The world spun. Laughter and applause echoed all around them. The sounds barely registered in her awe-filled mind. She closed her eyes and melted into his warm embrace. He held her as if she was the most precious, prized possession he could ever own. And she held him the same way.

A deep growl escaped Camden's throat once he finally pulled back. Her eyelids fluttered open and she drank in the sight of her handsome, beloved husband. His dark eyes burned with lust and love, excitement and relief. She never felt more wonderful than at that moment.

"May I present," the reverend drew the crowd's attention, "Lord Camden and Lady Susanna, Viscount and Viscountess Beckinworth."

As the crowd cheered, the newly-wed couple rushed from the hall. Ribbons and flower petals spiraled around them. Susanna and Camden stalled in the vestibule, directly under mistletoe. With a mischievous smile, he jerked her back into his embrace and kissed his wife. She returned his kiss with equal need and fervor. Ready for night to fall, ready to pleasure each other as only a husband and wife should, the moon couldn't rise quickly enough.

EPILOGUE

Northern Derbyshire, England

Five Years Later

Viscountess Susanna Beckinworth adored her husband's estate. The Beckinworth family moved to the area two centuries before and built a grand manor along a trout-filled stream. The estate was a massive amalgam of towering trees and heather moors. Nestled near the summit of a rolling mountain, the manor was in desperate need of a woman's touch, if not an upgrade, when she'd first moved in. After a few decorating adjustments, the manor felt like home.

The cotton spinning mill was larger than she expected. After spending several weeks reviewing various accounts, logs and books with every intention of helping her husband run the business, she realized he truly didn't need assistance. He turned a failing business into a prosperous one in only a few years. The upgrades, safety precautions and pay raises he established for the workers were extraordinary and nearly unheard of in the country. Still, he wanted her by his side during routine inspections and meetings with the mill's managers. He also wanted her to monitor the books.

That was until she became pregnant with their first child soon after the wedding. At first, he rarely restricted her activities, but once she started wobbling when descending staircases and eating enough for two grown men, he regulated her activities to simple sitting, light reading and relaxing. Her overprotective husband claimed toiling over mathematical books was too stressful and visiting the cramped millhouse too unhealthy for her delicate condition. She scoffed in his face but his adamant demands never wavered. Since she knew his demands stemmed from worry, she eventually agreed. Besides, once the baby was born, she wouldn't have much time for the millhouse, anyway.

Her sister, Beatrix, gave birth to a healthy son a few weeks before Susanna found out she was expecting. Bea and her husband were ecstatic. Assisting the midwife, what Susanna had witnessed as a child staring through a crack in a doorway did not compare to this new experience. The entire family was there for the birth, including her brothers and their wives—except Deandra.

Poor Beatrix admitted she slept with Lord Gaynor before she met her husband. She felt pressured into it, but did so willingly. She was infatuated with him. But once she married her own earl, she refused Gaynor's advances, to his angry dismay. He had harassed her just as he did Susanna for years. Unfortunately, both women were too embarrassed and worried to confess it. Now that Susanna knew, as did her parents and Camden, the sisters had grown much closer.

Beatrix's husband, however, remained oblivious. According to Bea, he cast aside his mistresses just a month before she gave birth for a monogamous relationship. Susanna prayed everything worked out.

Five years passed without a word from Lord Gaynor. Camden and her father spoke to him before the wedding and settled on a truce. Still, Gaynor wasn't the sort of man to keep his word. They still worried about a lawsuit—Camden had taken too many liberties in striking a man of higher social standing—though nothing ever came of it. Deandra, who occasionally visited Lorican Manor with her children, explained to her parents that she convinced her husband not to press charges because she believed Susanna and Beatrix would undoubtedly press charges against *him* in return. And while that would most assuredly tarnish her sisters' reputations, Lord Gaynor feared his own reputation would suffer in the scandal, as well. Even though Deandra accepted the truth that her husband harassed her sisters, she avoided them instead of making amends.

Susanna rested her hands over her rounded stomach and smiled. At least six months pregnant and due during the Christmas season, she hoped for a daughter this time. Relaxing in the library with several books scattered across an ornate desk and her four-year-old son sleeping on a sofa, she fondly remembered her wedding day.

Not surprisingly, the reception was a catastrophe.

A back door to the kitchen was left open and nearly a dozen squawking chicken and geese, covered in snow and slush, flocked into the dining room with wings flapping. The ensuing chase knocked over tables, chairs, food, presents and wedding guests. Susanna simply fell to the floor and laughed the whole time. Better to laugh than cry. Once the servants finally ushered the birds outside and back into the barn, Camden picked her up, both of them covered in feathers, and laughed. He had kissed her so thoroughly, in front of so many people that she silently thanked the birds for the mess.

The snow continued all day. She thought it would never cease, and that it would always be forever winter. Spending their wedding night in her bedchamber, they made love for hours. The snow ceased by morning and within three days the ice and snow melted enough for travel. The stranded wedding guests left as soon as possible. With careful preparation of the horses and carriage, the Beckinworths left for their honeymoon. Luckily, not a single mishap occurred in France.

As Susanna stared out a large window in the library, thunder boomed in the distance. Her little boy immediately woke and rushed to her side. He buried his face in her skirts just as two strong arms wrapped around her heavy stomach. Warmth seeped into her body. She relaxed into Camden's strong embrace and smiled.

Life was perfect. She wouldn't change a single thing.

ABOUT THE AUTHOR
AMBER DAULTON

My mind is a wonderland of romance and adventure, laughter and awesome ways of kicking a guy when he's down. I read and write contemporary, paranormal and historical romance novels alike. I just can't get enough of feisty heroines and alpha heroes. My wonderful husband supports me in my career and always lends a pair of eyes to my manuscripts. Writing takes up most of my time, aside from my tedious day job in the retail industry, and I probably wouldn't be too sane without my computer. After all, what's a girl to do when there are people jabbering away in her head and it's hard to shut them up? Write! Nothing else works.

58549256R00063

Made in the USA
Lexington, KY
13 December 2016